Isla saw the wolves' muscles bunch. They were about to spring! She tensed, and then suddenly a little unicorn came bursting out of the nearby trees and charged recklessly at the wolves. "Buttercup!" Isla shrieked, her head spinning. Whatever was her unicorn doing there?

UNICORN ACADEMY

...where magic happens!

HAVE YOU READ?

Sophia and Rainbow

Scarlett and Blaze

Ava and Star

Isabel and Cloud

Layla and Dancer

Olivia and Snowflake

Rosa and Crystal

Ariana and Whisper

Matilda and Pearl

Freya and Honey

Violet and Twinkle

Unicorn Academy
...Where magic happens!

Isla and Buttercup

Julie Sykes

illustrated by
Lucy Truman

nosy crow

To Isla Rose Nicole –
may all your days be filled with magic.

First published in the UK in 2020 by Nosy Crow Ltd
The Crow's Nest, 14 Baden Place, Crosby Row
London, SE1 1YW, UK

Nosy Crow and associated logos are trademarks and/or registered
trademarks of Nosy Crow Ltd

Text copyright © Julie Sykes and Linda Chapman, 2020
Illustrations copyright © Lucy Truman, 2020

Printed and bound in the UK by Clays Ltd, Elcograf S.p.A.

Papers used by Nosy Crow are made from wood grown in
sustainable forests.

ISBN: 978 1 78800 728 3

www.nosycrow.com

CHAPTER ONE

"Oh, wow! That's amazing, Matilda!" said Isla. Matilda from Diamond dorm had covered the back wall of the stable block with paper and was drawing an enormous mural that showed the last year at Unicorn Academy. There were pictures of everyone arriving; being paired with their unicorns; galloping through the grounds and camping in the woods. The other girls from Diamond dorm – Rosa, Freya, Ariana and Violet – were painting the background, while Unibot, the robotic unicorn that Freya had built, was helping the girls by trundling around with pots of paint.

"It does look good, doesn't it?" said Rosa.

Isla nodded. "I bet the parents will love it!"

Every student who'd bonded with their unicorn
– and discovered its magic power – was about to
graduate. In just a few days' time, all the students'
and unicorns' parents would come to the academy
for the graduation ball. Students who weren't

graduating, like Isla, would watch the ceremony, then go home for Christmas and return for a second year in January.

Matilda looked round. "Do you want to help us, Isla?"

Isla shook her head. "I'd only mess it up."

"Don't be silly, I'm no good at painting so I'm just doing the grass," said Violet. "Come and join me!"

It looked like fun but Isla didn't want to risk ruining their beautiful mural. "It's OK," she said cheerfully, "the others from my dorm will be here soon. We're making snowflakes to hang from the ceiling." She grinned. "That's about my level when it comes to art!"

"Come and sit with us anyway," said Violet, waving Isla over with a paintbrush.

Isla smiled again. "Thanks." The Diamond dorm girls were always so friendly to her. She was

going to miss them when they all graduated.

Her own dorm, Ruby dorm, didn't get on quite as well as Diamond dorm. Molly and Anna were nice but they were best friends who did everything together. The fourth member of Ruby dorm, Valentina, had rich parents who were governors at the school and she often acted as if she was better than everyone else.

I wonder who'll be in my dorm next year, Isla thought as she settled down to work on her snowflake. She wasn't sure how she felt about returning to the academy on her own and was glad that Buttercup, her confident, energetic little unicorn, would be with her.

"We've been trying to think of where Ms Willow could be hiding out," said Violet, including Isla in the conversation. "What do you think?"

Pretty, friendly Ms Willow had been the school nurse, until Diamond dorm had discovered that

she'd been draining magic from around the island as part of an evil plan to take it over! A month ago, Ms Willow had kidnapped Violet and her unicorn Twinkle, and had taken them to the Frozen Lagoon where she was storing all the magic in the water under the ice. Thanks to a tip-off from Isla, the Diamond dorm girls had gone to Violet and Twinkle's rescue, and they'd all escaped. Now Ms Willow had vanished without a trace.

"She might have gone back to the Frozen Lagoon," said Isla. Her face reddened as everyone turned to look at her. She hadn't meant to voice that thought aloud. Would they all think it was a stupid idea?

"Of course! That's a brilliant thought!" said Violet.

"You clever thing, Isla," said Matilda.

Isla, who found it embarrassing when anyone complimented her, turned even redder. "I don't

know. I bet everyone else has better ideas."

Rosa grinned at her, "You shouldn't always put yourself down. It's obvious when you think about it. Ms Willow is bound to be hiding at the Frozen Lagoon, she's got lots of magic stored there – the magic she has stolen from around the island – and it's a secret place that no one else knows how to get to."

"So, how do we catch her if she's there?" said Freya.

Just then Molly, Anna and Valentina arrived carrying paper and scissors.

"Ooh, I like your snowflake, Isla!" said Molly.

Anna nodded. "Can you show me how you made it and I'll do another one just the same?"

Isla felt a sudden tingle of happiness but it was quickly squashed by Valentina.

"It's too big," she declared, with a swish of her long, dark hair. "And it's wonky."

"Don't listen to her, Isla!" Rosa rounded on Valentina. "That was a really mean thing to say!"

Valentina looked surprised. "But the cutting out is wonky in parts."

"So? No one will notice at all when it's hanging up," said Freya.

"I actually think it'll be good to have snowflakes of all different sizes," added Molly.

"We've got some glue and glitter over here, Isla," Matilda called. "Why don't you start decorating the one you've made?"

"Can we help?" Anna asked Isla.

Anna and Molly fetched glue and glitter and sat down with Isla to decorate the snowflake.

Valentina gave them a cross look. "What about me?" she said, clearly feeling left out. "What am I going to do?"

No one answered her.

Valentina huffed and started to draw some

snowflakes on her own. Isla glanced over at her. She just didn't understand why Valentina said the things she did. If she wanted to have friends, why didn't she try harder to make people like her? Valentina was in her second year at the academy, and although her unicorn Golden Briar had discovered that he had wind magic, the two of them still hadn't bonded. Valentina would be the only student staying on for a third year.

I'd hate that, thought Isla, feeling a sudden rush of sympathy for her. *If it was me I'd do anything to graduate with everyone else.*

Just then, there was a clatter of hooves and the unicorns came trotting into the stables. They had been outside in the meadow, enjoying the winter sun.

"We want to go for a cross-country ride," Whisper, Ariana's handsome unicorn, announced.

"We won't have many more chances to all be together," said Honey, Freya's unicorn.

"Can we go too?" Buttercup asked, trotting over to Isla and nuzzling her as everyone started putting the art equipment down. Buttercup was a very pretty little unicorn with a pink, yellow and green mane and tail, and a sparkling white coat that was patterned with flowers. "There are some new cross-country jumps that I can't wait to try."

"They're not too high for you, are they?" Isla asked. Buttercup was one of the smallest unicorns.

"Nothing's too high for me!" Buttercup declared confidently.

The others were already leaving the stable block but Isla noticed that Freya was searching

the ground and Honey, her unicorn, was walking slowly around, her muzzle touching the floor.

"Have you lost something?" Isla asked.

"A tiny screw from Unibot." Freya pulled a face. "It's so small you'd hardly think it matters. But without it Unibot can't travel backwards. Look."

The robotic unicorn was now stuck in a corner, a basket of paint pots in its mouth.

"Buttercup and I will help you look," said Isla.

Buttercup nodded. She liked being helpful just as much as Isla did.

Freya smiled. "Thanks. It has to be here somewhere."

"*Find the screw, find it!*" Buttercup sang out while rapping a hoof in time to the beat.

There was a loud pop and Isla saw a pink spark drift down to the floor.

"Oh!" said Buttercup in surprise. "Did you see that? What was it?"

Isla and Buttercup

"Is it your magic?" said Freya in excitement. "The first time Honey found her super-speed, magic pink sparks came from her hooves."

"Do that again, whatever it was you were doing," urged Honey.

"What, this?" Buttercup thumped her hoof on the floor. "*Find the screw! Find—!*" she chanted, breaking off as a flurry of pink sparkles swirled up from her hooves.

Isla hardly dared to believe what she was seeing as the sparkles twirled and danced, then rose up together to form an arrow. It quivered in the air then dived, its tip pointing at a crack where the stable wall joined the floor.

Buttercup trotted over and peered into the crack. "Here's Freya's screw! I *did* find it!"

"You've got your magic!" squealed Isla, throwing her arms around Buttercup's neck. "It's finding magic!"

"Awesome!" said Freya. "You'll be able to find things whenever they get lost."

Buttercup's eyes shone. "Let's go and tell the others straight away!"

CHAPTER TWO

Freya and Isla vaulted on to their unicorns and galloped after the others. Isla was buzzing with excitement and couldn't wait to share the news that Buttercup had found her magic.

"Wait!" Buttercup whinnied to the other unicorns.

They slowed to a halt.

"What's up?" demanded Rosa. A look of alarm crossed her face. "It's not Ms Willow, is it?"

"No, it's not Ms Willow," said Freya.

"What is it then?" said Violet.

"It's Buttercup!" Isla burst out. "She's just

discovered her magic!"

She told them what had happened.

"It was amazing!" enthused Freya. "A magical arrow appeared in the air and pointed to where the missing screw was."

"I'm so pleased, Isla!" Violet exclaimed.

"Finding magic's so cool!" said Isla, thinking of all the people she and Buttercup could help.

Valentina frowned. "Don't think that just because you've found Buttercup's magic you'll be able to graduate!" she snapped. "You've still got to bond, remember! Come on, Golden Briar. Let's go."

"But..." Golden Briar started to protest.

"Now!" exclaimed Valentina, clapping her heels against his sides. With a sigh, Golden Briar cantered away.

"She's so mean," said Matilda. "She could at least have congratulated you."

"Take no notice of her," said Violet. "I bet you'll bond really quickly and be able to graduate after all."

"Yep!" Buttercup declared happily. "I bet we will too."

Isla patted Buttercup's neck as they rode on. She was very glad that her unicorn wasn't upset by Valentina's comments but she couldn't help feeling a little deflated. She'd been so excited to find Buttercup's magic but of course they still might not graduate. *Oh, I hope we bond soon,* she thought. *I really do!*

★

They all had a great time on the cross-country course and returned to the stables chattering and laughing. Golden Briar was already in his stall, next door to Buttercup's.

"Did you have fun?" he asked.

Buttercup nodded. "It was amazing! I jumped

a huge log pile."

"I wish I'd been able to come with you," said Golden Briar.

"Next time you must. Tell Valentina it's your turn to decide what you do. Isn't that right, Isla?" said Buttercup.

"Valentina often lets me do what I want," Golden Briar said firmly. He turned back to his hay net to show that the conversation was over.

Isla suddenly felt sorry for Golden Briar – and for Valentina too. How would it feel not to have bonded after two years at the academy?

"Buttercup!" Matilda called out. "Can you use your magic to help me find my favourite blue pen? I lost it last week."

Buttercup lifted her head. "Coming!" She and Isla went to the Diamond dorm aisle. "Stand back, everyone!" Buttercup gave a theatrical bow, clearly enjoying herself. She lifted her hoof, then smacked it down on the ground. "Find Matilda's blue pen!"

Everyone gasped as a rainbow of sparks shot up and arched above her head. The arrow hung in the air for a second, then shimmied its tail and darted out through the stable door.

"After it!" cried Buttercup. She cantered out of the stable then skidded to a halt. "Whoops! Sorry, Isla! I almost forgot you!" Isla ran up to her and vaulted on. The others mounted their unicorns and cantered after the arrow.

It sailed over the stable roof and into the meadow, stopping by the stream. Buttercup trotted over to where the arrow hovered in the air, pointing at the reeds.

"I've found your pen!" she exclaimed. She thrust her muzzle into the reeds.

CLUCK!

With a flurry of wings a pale blue bird burst

indignantly from the reeds.

"Whaaa!" cried Buttercup, staggering backwards in shock.

Rosa burst out laughing. "Your magic found a blue *hen* not Matilda's blue *pen*, Buttercup!"

Isla turned hot with embarrassment for Buttercup as everyone rocked with laughter, but Buttercup laughed just as loudly as the others.

"Oh dear!" she snorted. "I think I need to practise a bit more."

"Don't worry," said Violet kindly. "Most unicorns find it hard to control their magic properly when they first discover their powers."

Matilda's unicorn, Pearl, nodded in agreement. "I found it really hard to hold glamours at first."

The other unicorns nodded too. "You get tired easily as well," said Twinkle. "But it gets better the more you practise."

"I'll practise lots then!" declared Buttercup. She nuzzled Isla. "You'll help me, won't you?"

"Of course," said Isla, leaning in to bury her face in Buttercup's long pink, yellow and green mane. When they bonded, a strand of her brown hair would turn the same colours. *Oh, please make that happen soon,* Isla thought again.

CHAPTER THREE

After lunch, Isla went to find Ms Nettles to tell her about Buttercup's finding magic. The head teacher's study door was shut and there was no answer when Isla knocked. Ms Rosemary, the Care of Unicorns teacher, looked out of her room. "Are you looking for Ms Nettles, Isla?"

Isla nodded. "Buttercup found her magic this morning."

"That's wonderful news!" said Ms Rosemary, beaming. "But I'm afraid Ms Nettles was called away last night on urgent business. I'm sure she'll be delighted to hear about Buttercup's magic when she gets back though."

Isla smiled and headed to the stables.

"Can we practise my magic?" asked Buttercup when she arrived. "Pleeeeeeease!" she added, fluttering her eyelashes.

Isla grinned. "Of course we can."

"Yay! Miki lost his ball last week and Golden Briar wants me to find Valentina's favourite scarf, and Monsoon said Ms Bramble lost—"

"Whoa!" said Isla, holding her hands up. "Maybe we should just find one thing at a time!"

"Oh, OK," Buttercup said with a huff. "We'll start with Miki's ball then. He was on the sports field when he lost it."

They went out to the sports field. Buttercup took a deep breath. "Miki's ball!" she exclaimed. "Find it!" A glittering arrow formed. It looped the loop then darted away.

"My magic's working! Yippee!" said Buttercup

as she raced after it.

The arrow flew in the direction of Sparkle Lake but as it got closer it whizzed from side to side as if it couldn't decide which way to go. Buttercup galloped after it. Isla began to feel alarmed. "Slow down, Buttercup!" she cried.

The arrow flew over the fountain then darted to the right and pointed at some rushes close to the bank. It stayed there for a second then it shot to a nearby bush before flying back to the fountain.

Buttercup pricked her ears and increased her speed.

"No, Buttercup!" Isla gasped. "We can't follow it into the lake! Stop!"

The arrow suddenly returned to the bush. Buttercup swerved to go after it but she was galloping too fast. Her hooves slid from under her. Isla shrieked as they skidded towards the multicoloured water.

Isla and Buttercup

SPLASH!

Buttercup's hooves hit the lake and a tidal wave of ice cold water splashed over them. Luckily Buttercup just managed to stop herself falling in completely.

"Whoops!" Buttercup regained her balance. "Are you OK, Isla?"

"Well, I'm pretty wet," said Isla, shivering. She had water dripping from the ends of her hair and droplets were already freezing on her clothes.

"Sorry!" said Buttercup sheepishly. "I was just trying to catch up with the arrow." She looked around. "Oh, it's gone," she said in disappointment.

"Why was it jumping around like that?" Isla asked.

"I don't know. It pointed at the bush before it vanished. Maybe Miki's ball is there." Buttercup trotted towards it.

"Wait! There's something in those rushes," said Isla, spotting a flash of colour.

Buttercup went over. "Valentina's scarf!" she said, pulling the scarf out of the rushes with her teeth. Isla leant over her neck and took it from her.

"Valentina will be happy to have it back. I wonder why the arrow pointed to it when we were looking for Miki's ball."

Buttercup frowned. "I guess I was thinking about both things at the same time – the ball and the scarf. Maybe it confused my magic. Let's see if there's anything in the bush."

She cantered over. "Miki's ball! Hooray!" Buttercup nudged it out with her nose.

"Aren't I clever? I found both things!"

Isla hesitated. She didn't want to hurt Buttercup's feelings. "That's great but you need to practise controlling your magic. Perhaps you should concentrate on one thing at a time?"

"I think I did very well," said Buttercup, slightly huffily.

Isla patted her neck. "You did, but let's start with small things first."

"I don't need to," Buttercup declared confidently. "I'm super good already!"

"Let's go and get you some sky berries," said Isla, changing the subject. Doing magic sapped a unicorn's strength and sky berries helped them to recover.

"OK, I guess I am a bit tired," admitted Buttercup.

They headed back to the stables. As they passed the play park, they saw Rosa, Matilda, Freya,

Ariana, Violet and their unicorns in a huddle by the swings.

"Shall we say hello?" said Buttercup.

Isla wasn't sure. "It looks like they might be having a private talk."

"So? They'll want to see us!" said Buttercup confidently. "They're our friends!" She cantered over.

"Hi, everyone! What are you talking about?" she whinnied.

Isla cringed. "It's OK," she said quickly. "You don't have to tell us if it's a secret."

"Don't be silly. We haven't got secrets from you two," said Violet. "We were just talking again about how we might find Ms Willow."

Rosa looked at them thoughtfully. "Buttercup, do you think you could use your magic to find her?"

"I bet I could," said Buttercup.

"Brilliant!" said Rosa. "Will you try?"

Buttercup nodded eagerly.

"Are you sure, Buttercup?" Isla asked. "I think you should practise some more and wait until you're not so tired before you try something so difficult."

Buttercup looked hurt. "Don't you believe in me, Isla?"

"Yes, but—"

"I found the ball and scarf, didn't I?" interrupted Buttercup.

"Yes, but we did almost fall into the lake!" Isla reminded her.

"That was just a silly mistake." Buttercup looked cross now.

"Maybe this isn't such a good idea, after all," said Ariana doubtfully. "Ms Willow is very clever. After all, she captured Prancer and they're a spell weaver." A spell weaver was the most powerful of

unicorns. Ms Willow had plaited binding ribbons into Prancer's mane to force her to do whatever she commanded. "It could be dangerous."

"It'll be fine!" Buttercup tossed her mane. "I know I can do it. Just watch and see!"

Buttercup struck the ground with her hoof. "Find Ms Willow!"

A few sparks spun in the air. They fizzled away.

"Find her!" Buttercup repeated, stamping both hooves so enthusiastically that she dislodged a clod of mud that shot up and splattered her in the

face. Violet giggled. "Find her!" said Buttercup once more, but this time no sparks appeared at all.

"Oh."Buttercup looked disappointed.

Isla felt awful for her.

Violet gave her a kind look. "Don't worry, Buttercup. Isla's right, you're probably too tired after finding all the other stuff."

"Maybe I do need sky berries to get my strength back," Buttercup said grudgingly.

"Let's go back to school now and we can try again tomorrow," said Rosa.

CHAPTER FOUR

"Sky berries for all the unicorns and hot chocolate for us!' said Matilda happily.

"I've got some marshmallows for the hot chocolate," said Ariana.

"You'll come and have some hot chocolate with us, won't you, Isla?" Violet said.

Isla glowed with pleasure at being included. "Yes please!"

They rode back to the stables in a noisy, chattering group. Isla was happy to be with everyone but she had an anxious feeling that Buttercup was cross with her.

Isla and Buttercup

I didn't mean to hurt her feelings, Isla thought. *I just didn't want her to look silly in front of everyone.*

"Isn't that Valentina?" said Freya, interrupting Isla's thoughts. "Where's she going?"

"Let's give her scarf back," said Isla. "I bet she'll be really pleased we found it for her." Buttercup cantered towards Golden Briar.

"Valentina!" called Isla.

"Go away!" Valentina shouted back.

"But I've got something of yours."

"What is it?" demanded Valentina, halting Golden Briar.

Isla took the scarf out of her pocket. "Buttercup used her magic to find it."

Valentina took the scarf from Isla and stuffed it in her pocket. She didn't even say thank you.

"Where are you going?" asked Isla curiously.

"None of your business!" snapped Valentina, and she rode away without another word.

"I was only trying to help," Isla said to Buttercup as they headed back to the stables.

"Well, not everyone wants your help," said Buttercup irritably. "I felt really stupid earlier when you said my magic wouldn't work."

"But I was right," Isla pointed out. "You were too tired."

"So what? It's better to try something and fail than not to try at all."

Isla wasn't sure she agreed. Surely it was better not to try if you thought you might get it wrong?

They lapsed into an awkward silence. Isla hadn't meant to upset Buttercup. She'd only tried to stop her using her magic because she knew that if *she'd* tried something and got it wrong, she'd be really embarrassed. Buttercup was different, though. She didn't mind making mistakes. *It's one of the things I love about her,* Isla realised. *She's so confident, she doesn't care what people think.*

Isla and Buttercup

As they reached the stables, Isla stroked Buttercup's neck. "I'm sorry. I didn't mean to make you feel silly. You're right. It is better to have a go at things and not be too cowardly to try, like me."

Buttercup nuzzled her. "You're not a coward, Isla. You just worry too much. I'm really glad we're paired together."

"Me too." Isla kissed her then fetched a bucket full of juicy sky berries.

Buttercup gave her a friendly nudge.

"Friends again?" Isla said hopefully.

"Always friends," said Buttercup.

Isla hugged her, feeling much more cheerful.

★

Isla had fun with the others in Diamond dorm over hot chocolate, and she was bursting with happiness as she ran back to Ruby dorm to get ready for dinner. The only person in there was Valentina. She was reading a letter and frowning.

"News from home?" Isla asked.

Valentina shook her head and shoved the letter into her chest of drawers, dropping the envelope in her haste. Isla picked it up for her. It had Valentina's name on it in swirly handwriting, and no other address.

Valentina snatched it from her and slammed the drawer shut. She sat on her bed as Isla changed into a clean hoodie and pulled a brush through her short hair.

"Aren't you going down to dinner?" Isla asked.

"I'm waiting for you," said Valentina.

Isla blinked. Valentina never usually waited for anyone. A thought crossed her mind. *Maybe Valentina was worried she would read her letter. Was it from a secret admirer or something?*

"I'm not ready," said Isla, deciding to test her theory.

"How long does it take to brush your hair?" Valentina retorted. "Hurry up. All of Ruby dorm looks bad if one of us is late." She went to snatch the hairbrush away but Isla held on to it.

"I said I'm not ready yet," Isla insisted.

Valentina glared at her. "You're so annoying."

Isla continued to slowly brush her hair while Valentina waited, her foot tapping impatiently on the floor.

Interesting, thought Isla. Valentina usually flounced off if she didn't get her way. What exactly was she hiding?

CHAPTER FIVE

Isla and Buttercup had arranged to meet Diamond dorm in the barn next to the stables before breakfast to try Buttercup's finding magic again. When Isla woke, Molly and Anna were still sleeping but Valentina's bed was empty. Where was she?

As Isla left the dorm, she spotted a white envelope on the floor that had been pushed under their door. It had Valentina's name on it, in exactly the same handwriting as the one from the day before.

Isla's eyes widened. Did Valentina have a

boyfriend? Was that who the letters were from? Biting back a giggle, she put the envelope on Valentina's bedside table.

As Isla headed for the Ruby dorm stables, Valentina poked her head out of Golden Briar's stall. "What are you doing here?" she asked.

"Oh ... I'm just doing something with Diamond dorm," Isla said vaguely.

"Is it time already?" Buttercup asked, looking over her stall door.

"Is it time for what?" said Valentina.

"Nothing," said Isla firmly. "Nothing at all."

"Ready when you are, Isla!" called Rosa.

Isla got Buttercup out of her stable.

Valentina followed them up the aisle. "What are you all doing? Can I come too?" she asked.

"No," Rosa spoke bluntly. "You don't like us and we don't much like you either."

Isla wished Rosa hadn't been quite so harsh,

but Valentina had been unkind to Matilda in the past and Rosa was a loyal friend.

"Fine!" Valentina barked. "I bet you're all doing something stupid anyway!" She stomped back into Golden Briar's stall.

Isla joined the others as they cantered to the barn.

"Are you ready to do your magic, Buttercup?" Matilda said.

"Definitely!" said Buttercup. "It's going to work this time, I just know it is!"

"Go, Buttercup!" said Ariana.

"Stand back, everyone," said Buttercup, clearly loving being the centre of attention. "Here goes!"

She struck the ground dramatically. "Find Ms Willow!" Sparks engulfed her hoof, twirling up in the air to form a quivering, coloured arrow.

Matilda squealed in excitement.

Buttercup shot Isla a smug look as the arrow floated towards the barn door.

"Go!" cried Isla, leaping on Buttercup's back, as the arrow began to gather speed.

She heard the whoops and cries of the others as they thundered behind her. Isla leaned forward, enjoying the wind on her face as they galloped.

"Where's it going?" she cried to Buttercup as the arrow headed out towards the vegetable gardens.

"I don't know!" said Buttercup.

The arrow reached a large compost heap that stood beside a dilapidated brick outbuilding at the bottom of the garden. It had a tree beside it, with branches that drooped down gracefully to the ground. The door was slightly ajar. The arrow hovered above the shed, pointing at it.

Buttercup skidded to a halt.

"Why's the arrow pointing at the shed?" said Rosa.

Freya caught her breath. "Maybe Ms Willow is inside!"

They all looked at each other in alarm.

"What should we do?" whispered Matilda.

Just then, the door moved. They all froze. Something the size of an apple with eight legs and googly eyes came scuttling out. Ariana shrieked but the rest of them sighed with relief.

"It's just a cave spider!" exclaimed Violet as the spider ran past them and up the tree trunk.

"The tree!" Freya pointed. "It's a weeping willow. That must be why the arrow brought us here. Buttercup, you found a *willow tree*, not Ms Willow!"

Isla and Buttercup

They all burst out laughing.

"Whoops!" said Buttercup.

"What's going on here, girls?"

Ms Nettles emerged from the shed, her glasses rattling on the end of her bony nose. The arrow exploded in a shower of sparkles that faded like a spent firework.

The girls stopped laughing instantly as the head teacher looked at them sternly, one hand on her hip. "Ms Nettles!" Rosa gasped in shock.

"Why are you all up so early?" Ms Nettles asked.

"Erm... We were ... out looking for sparkle moss," Matilda invented.

Violet nodded furiously. "To decorate the ballroom for graduation day."

Ms Nettles frowned. "Sparkle moss grows near water. I would try by the lake and stay away from here. This building isn't safe."

"We'll go to the lake right away," said Freya.

Isla remembered something. "Ms Nettles, Buttercup's got finding magic!" she said excitedly.

"Really?" said Ms Nettles, raising her eyebrows. "Well, if her magic brought her here to find sparkle moss, she clearly needs more practice." She shooed at them with her hands. "Go on. Away with you all."

Isla's face fell and she saw Buttercup's ears droop.

"She could at least have said well done," said

Violet indignantly, as they walked away.

"We probably just caught her at a bad time," said Isla, but she couldn't help feeling upset that Ms Nettles hadn't seemed more pleased for her and Buttercup. "I didn't even realise she'd got back. Ms Rosemary said she'd been called away on urgent business. I wonder why she was in the shed?"

"Studying the cave spider maybe," said Freya. "She does love nature."

"Or collecting more beetles," added Violet. Ms Nettles had a large collection of beetles.

Ariana shuddered. "I don't understand why anyone would want to collect beetles!"

"I like beetles," said Whisper, Ariana's unicorn. Whisper had soothing magic and loved all animals.

At Sparkle Lake they collected some sparkle moss, just in case Ms Nettles checked up on them,

before returning to the stables. As Isla passed Golden Briar's stall, she heard Valentina talking to him in a low voice.

"I don't know what to do. The person writing them says they need my help. This might be mad but I think the writer might be—" She broke off abruptly as she saw Isla and Buttercup.

"Were you listening to our private conversation?" Valentina demanded.

For a second Isla thought she saw a flash of fear in Valentina's eyes. "No!" she said. "Of course I wasn't!" She wondered why Valentina looked so worried about being overheard. Who did she think was sending her the letters? A horrible suspicion suddenly filled Isla's mind. Could it be Ms Willow? Why else would Valentina look so guilty and anxious?

Valentina pointed at the moss Isla was carrying. "You were up early just to collect sparkle moss?"

"No, we didn't set out to just get moss," said Isla, without thinking. Too late, she realised she'd said too much.

"Why *were* you out so early then?" Valentina asked. "What were you and Diamond dorm doing?"

"Um..." Isla stammered. "It was um ... nothing."

"Tell me!" demanded Valentina. She lowered her voice again. "Is it something to do with Ms Willow?"

Isla's heart hammered. What had made Valentina jump to that conclusion? Maybe her suspicions about the writer of Valentina's mysterious letters *were* correct! "Ms Willow? No!" she burst out, hoping she sounded convincing.

"If it is, I want to help," said Valentina, her voice suddenly intense. "I really do. Tell me what's going on. *Please!*"

Isla opened and shut her mouth. She hated leaving Valentina out but she didn't quite trust her, and anyway, the secret wasn't hers to tell. "I ... I can't say," she stammered.

Valentina's face hardened. "Fine! Be like that then! If you don't want my help then you shan't have it!" She left the stable and stomped away.

CHAPTER SIX

After lunch, Isla met with Diamond dorm in the barn. She'd been thinking over and over about her conversation with Valentina and what she'd heard Valentina saying to Golden Briar. She had a very bad feeling. She wondered whether to say anything to the others but she had no proof that the letters Valentina was getting were from Ms Willow. It was just a suspicion. What if she told them and it wasn't true? She'd look so stupid!

"So, how *are* we going to find Ms Willow?" said Freya. "If she is at the Frozen Lagoon, she's going to be practically impossible to find. No one knows its exact location and it's not marked on the Magic Map."

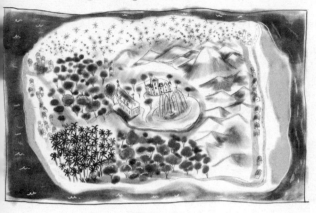

The Magic Map was an exact replica of Unicorn Island that was kept in the Great Hall. If the map thought you wanted to help, it would magically transport you anywhere on the island that you asked it to.

"We could use my magic again?" suggested Buttercup. "I could ask it to find the Frozen Lagoon."

"You could," said Ariana carefully. "But if the Magic Map isn't powerful enough to show us where the Frozen Lagoon is then I'm not sure your magic will be able to help, Buttercup."

Buttercup looked indignant. "Don't you think I can find Ms Willow?"

"Maybe you should practise a bit more first," said Violet quickly. "Soon your magic will be stronger and then you can try again."

"If there's time," said Freya. "We've only got a couple of days left until graduation."

"We need another plan," said Rosa.

They threw around suggestions but by the end of lunchtime they still didn't have any idea of how to get to the Frozen Lagoon. Isla went back to her dorm to get ready for her afternoon lessons and saw another envelope lying on Valentina's bed.

Isla picked the envelope up curiously and glanced across at Valentina's drawer. It was half open and she could see other letters inside. She knew she shouldn't look but no one was around. What if they *were* from Ms Willow? *I'll just look at a few lines*, Isla thought. Feeling guilty for prying but too worried not to look, Isla picked up the top letter and scanned it.

You're so much smarter than all the other students, Valentina. You understand how things work. You know I want to make Unicorn Island great and you are the one student who I believe can help me. In return, I will help you and Golden Briar graduate. Think about it, Valentina. That is what you want most in the world, isn't it?

There was no name or signature on the bottom.

Hearing footsteps on the stairs, Isla shoved the letter back in the drawer and ran to her bed. She picked up her hairbrush as Molly, Anna and Valentina walked in. Isla's mind spun round and round. Who were the letters from and what did they mean?

Valentina picked up the new envelope from her pillow. She quickly opened and read it, then shoved it into her drawer with the others. Then she sat down on her bed, facing away from Isla.

"Are you OK?" asked Isla.

"Why wouldn't I be?" Valentina said sharply.

"Who was your letter from?"

"None of your business!" Valentina glared at her. "You won't share your secrets with me so I won't share mine with you!"

Not fair! thought Isla, stung. *I'm trying to protect Unicorn Island. Can you say the same?*

The bell rang and everyone left together to go to afternoon lessons. Isla pretended that she'd forgotten her pencil case and ran back to the dorm. When she got there, she pulled out the letter Valentina had just received from the top of the pile. It simply read:

Tonight, I want to help you. It is time to prove your loyalty.

A feeling of foreboding shivered down Isla's spine. *What should I do?* she thought. *If I tell the others, they might confront Valentina and she'll know I've*

read her letters. And what if it's nothing? I'll have falsely accused Valentina of something bad...

Isla hesitated a moment longer, before pushing the letter back in the drawer and running to her lesson.

Later, as Isla got ready to practise the drill ride her dorm would perform in front of the parents, she watched Valentina through the partition that separated Buttercup's stable from Golden Briar's. Valentina was whispering and Golden Briar was shaking his head emphatically. Isla moved closer to the partition.

"We've got to go, Golden Briar," she heard Valentina plead.

"No, Valentina, we can't!"

"But this could be our only chance to—"

"What's up, Isla?" Buttercup called out. "Why are you standing over there?"

"No reason," said Isla, hurrying back to her.

Isla and Buttercup

She thought about what Valentina had said: *We've got to go.* Go where? She bit her lip. If the letters were from Ms Willow, did that mean Valentina was planning on meeting with her? Another shiver ran down her spine as she remembered the letter she had read: *Tonight, I want to help you. It is time to prove your loyalty.*

"Are you sure you're all right?" Buttercup nudged her. "You seem distracted."

Isla bit her lip. "Buttercup, if you suspected someone was going to make a really big mistake would it be right to tell your friends? Even if there was a chance you were wrong and might be falsely accusing that person, as well as making yourself look stupid?" Isla suddenly realised she trusted Buttercup's opinion. They were very different but together that made them stronger.

"You should definitely tell your friends," said Buttercup immediately. "Imagine if you didn't and

something bad happened as a result. You'd feel awful. If the person has nothing to hide then they shouldn't mind explaining themselves. I think it's better to risk looking silly than to let someone make a big mistake."

Isla hugged her. "You're right. Thank you. I'm so lucky to have you as my unicorn."

"And I'm lucky to have you as my rider!" Buttercup said, nuzzling her.

CHAPTER SEVEN

Isla and Buttercup left the stables to go to the drill ride practice.

I'll tell Diamond dorm about Valentina's letters just as soon as I get a chance to speak to them on their own, thought Isla.

Diamond dorm were ahead of her, laughing with the boys from Topaz dorm as Matilda and Miki tried to trip each other up.

Ms Nettles came marching towards the stables. "Matilda! Stop that this instant!" she shouted.

"Sorry, Miss," said Matilda, giving her an apologetic grin as Miki stumbled.

"It was my fault too, sorry, Miss," said Miki.

Ms Nettles ignored him. "Matilda, you will not ride this afternoon. Instead you'll write out a hundred lines saying *I must behave more appropriately*."

Matilda gaped in shock. "But ... I said sorry and we're about to practise the drill ride..."

"Silence or I shall make that two hundred lines!"

Isla and Violet exchanged astonished looks. The teachers were all uptight about finding Ms Willow, especially Ms Nettles, but she was never usually so fierce or unfair. Matilda looked close to tears.

"Please, Ms Nettles. We've so little time left to practice," Rosa begged. "Can't Matilda do lines later?"

"One hundred lines for the whole of Diamond dorm!" Ms Nettles barked.

Everyone gasped.

Ms Nettles looked around. "Anyone else?" she enquired. No one dared to move. She nodded. "Diamond dorm, take your unicorns back and go inside now. The rest of you get on with your practise. Oh, and Valentina?"

"Yes?" Valentina looked at her warily. Ms Nettles was her aunt, but she never showed Valentina any special favours.

"I would like you to have a starring role in the drill ride."

Valentina blinked. "But I'm not ready to graduate." Isla knew that at the start of the year, Valentina would have loved to have a main role.

Now she looked almost upset. "Shouldn't I just do what everyone else does?" Valentina went on.

Ms Nettles smiled at her. "Always so modest, Valentina. No, you deserve this role. Come to my study straight after dinner and we'll have a quick chat about it." She turned and strode away.

As soon as Ms Nettles was out of earshot everyone started to talk at once.

"What's going on?" hissed Himmat from Topaz dorm. "I've never known the Nettle Patch to be so prickly!"

"It's not fair," said Miki. "I'm as much to blame as Matilda and Ms Nettles didn't give me lines."

"I'm sure she'll give you some if you want," said Jake with a grin. "Just go and ask her."

"Maybe not," said Miki, rolling his eyes. "But I do feel bad for Diamond dorm."

Isla glanced at Valentina. Did *she* know why her aunt was in such a bad mood? Valentina looked up.

"What are you staring at?" she demanded.

"Nothing," Isla said hurriedly.

★

When afternoon lessons were over, Isla went to the barn to meet up with Diamond dorm. "Did you get your lines done?" she asked them.

They all nodded.

"I still don't understand why Ms Nettles was so mean," said Violet.

"It was very weird," Rosa agreed, "but we're here to discuss Ms Willow and how we're going to find her. We're running out of time."

Isla felt suddenly hot. This was her moment to tell the others about Valentina's letters and the conversation she'd overheard between Valentina and Golden Briar. But now the moment was here, doubts filled her mind again. What if she'd made a huge mistake? She'd look like a complete idiot!

"The good thing is, Ms Willow can't get into the

school grounds," said Ariana. "The teachers have put protection spells on the boundaries to keep her out."

Isla hesitated. If Ms Willow couldn't get into the grounds then how could Valentina be planning on meeting her? Ms Willow couldn't be the mystery letter writer. Isla swallowed and kept silent.

★

After dinner, Isla left the table at the same time as Valentina.

"We're going to the barn with the unicorns," said Violet, as Isla passed her. "Are you coming?"

"I'll join you in a bit," said Isla. Valentina had been unusually quiet over dinner and she wanted to see if she could find out why. Maybe she'd had another letter?

As Isla followed Valentina up the stairs, Ms Nettles appeared. "There you are, Valentina. Are you ready for our meeting? I hope so. Tonight, I want to help you."

Isla and Buttercup

Valentina smiled as she and Ms Nettles went down the teachers' corridor together. Something bothered Isla as she watched them. What was it?

Tonight, I want to help you.

The words echoed in her head. They were the exact same ones that had been written in Valentina's mystery letters. Could it be a coincidence? Surely Ms Nettles couldn't be the letter writer, could she?

Isla hurried along the corridor, tiptoeing the last few metres up to Ms Nettles' study. The door was slightly ajar and she could hear Valentina's voice.

"You might as well stop pretending. I know you're not my aunt!" she heard her say.

Isla's eyes widened.

"Clever girl," a voice purred. "I knew I was right to trust you and send you those letters! You're so much smarter than everyone else, Valentina. How did I give myself away?"

"My aunt would never show any favouritism to me like you did over the graduation display ride," said Valentina. "So, who are you?"

There was a faint flash of light. Isla pressed her eye to the crack in the door and smothered a squeak. Ms Willow was suddenly standing in Ms Nettles' study!

CHAPTER EIGHT

"Ms Willow!" exclaimed Valentina triumphantly. "I knew I was right. I suspected that you sent the letters and when my aunt started behaving strangely today, I guessed it wasn't really her but you in disguise!" Isla was astonished that she didn't sound scared. "How did you disguise yourself and get around the protection spells?" Valentina asked.

"Prancer cast a glamour, making me look like Ms Nettles. As for the protection spells —" Ms Willow waved a hand — "with the magic I've stored in the lagoon and with Prancer's powers,

they were easy to break."

"Where is my aunt?" asked Valentina, and now Isla was sure she heard a tremor in her voice.

"Safely out of the way, imprisoned in a secret place. I sent her a letter inviting her to an urgent meeting about Ms Willow and as she rode out of the school, I captured her and her unicorn. Now I shall I bind all the unicorns in this school to me and then they shall become my army and help me take over the island!"

"How?" said Valentina.

Ms Willow laughed and clasped her hands in delight. "A girl after my own heart. Always asking questions. There is enough magic stored in the Frozen Lagoon to make binding ribbons for every unicorn at the academy. Once the ribbons are in their manes they will obey me, just as Prancer does!"

Isla's heart clenched as Valentina chuckled slyly. "So where do I come into all of this and, more importantly, what do I get in return?"

"Money, power and of course you'll get to graduate from the academy. Not that you'll need to after tomorrow night. First, you must prove your loyalty by binding Golden Briar to you. Then we shall work together to bind all the unicorns. We can do this if we work together. What do you say?"

Say no, Isla thought fiercely. *Don't agree!*

Her stomach sank as she heard Valentina say firmly, "Yes, I'll do it."

"I knew I had made the right choice!" said Ms Willow. "Fetch Golden Briar, then meet me by the

lake. Do not breathe a word of this to anyone, especially not Golden Briar. Once he is bound to you, my quest – *our* quest – to take over the Unicorn Island will begin!"

Isla didn't stop to listen any more. She raced back along the corridor and up to the teachers' lounge, but as she got closer her courage failed. What if none of the teachers believed her? She didn't have any proof. They might just shoo her away or, even worse, they might laugh at her.

So, what should she do? Diamond dorm! If she told them, they would help convince the teachers. She was sure of it! Remembering that they were going to the barn, Isla charged back along the corridor and out into the dark night. As she got closer to the barn, she heard laughter coming from it. She had just reached the door when she caught a movement from the corner of her eye – it was Valentina leading Golden Briar out of the stable block.

Isla felt a rush of fierce anger. How could Valentina be so evil as to work with Ms Willow?

"Valentina!" she yelled furiously, changing direction and running straight towards her dorm-mate. But Valentina didn't hear her. She vaulted on to Golden Briar's back and cantered straight towards the lake – and Ms Willow.

Isla charged after her, as fast as she could. "Valentina! No!" she screamed.

CHAPTER NINE

Isla ran faster than she'd ever run in her life. *I have to stop Valentina.* The thought drummed through her brain, over and over again. Getting closer to the lake, Isla saw Ms Willow on a tall unicorn with a golden mane. Golden Briar had stopped next to Ms Willow's unicorn, and Ms Willow was smiling at Valentina and reaching for her hand.

"Come with me, my dear."

"I didn't realise we were going somewhere." Isla thought she could hear an edge to Valentina's voice, a sudden quiver of concern. "Where are

you taking me?"

"To the Frozen Lagoon!" Ms Willow's fingers closed on Valentina's.

"No!" shrieked Isla, bursting out of the shadows and grabbing Valentina's foot.

For a second, she saw Valentina and Ms Willow's shocked faces, and then there was a flash of green and the world fell away. Isla hung on to Valentina with all her strength. She spun round and round and then suddenly dropped to the ground, landing with a thud on a glassy, freezing surface. The sky was packed with glittering stars. Isla blinked, realising she was on a thick layer of ice above a lagoon that swirled eerily beneath it. This had to be the mysterious Frozen Lagoon where Ms Willow was storing the magic stolen from the island. Isla scrambled towards the bank.

"You!" Ms Willow hissed. "What are *you* doing here?" She swung round to Valentina. "Did you

tell her about meeting me?"

"No!" Valentina exclaimed, looking at Isla in astonishment.

Ms Willow flicked a bolt of magic at Isla. Isla cried out in pain as it smacked into her and sent her flying backwards across the lagoon. As she landed all the breath was knocked out of her.

"Isla!" she heard Valentina cry.

"Ignore her!" snapped Ms Willow. "She is no threat to us. I'll deal with her in a minute. Prancer, make sure she does not leave the ice until I am back." The golden-maned unicorn nodded obediently. "I'll go and fetch the ribbons so that you can bind Golden Briar to prove your loyalty."

It was Valentina's turn to nod, and Isla felt a rush of hatred as Ms Willow stalked away towards a hut near the lagoon.

As soon as Ms Willow disappeared inside, Valentina slid from Golden Briar's back. She

looked briefly towards where Isla was scrambling to her feet and then ran over to Prancer. Pulling something from her pocket, she grabbed Prancer's mane. Isla saw a flash of moonlight on metal.

"Valentina! Stop! Don't, whatever you're doing! You mustn't help Ms Willow!" she cried.

"Help Ms Willow!" Valentina spluttered. "For goodness sake, Isla! As if I would!"

"What? You can't deny it!" said Isla. "She's getting the binding ribbons right now!"

"I had to agree so I could do this!" Valentina held up a pair of scissors triumphantly and a clump of ribbons fell to the ground. "It was my plan all along."

"I'm free of the binding!" whinnied Prancer, shaking her mane. "The ribbons are gone! Oh, thank you, Valentina!"

"Did you really believe that I would bind Golden Briar to me?" Valentina exclaimed. "I'd never do that!"

"Oh!" Isla's eyes were wide as she scrambled off the ice. "So, you aren't in league with Ms Willow?"

"Don't be silly! I was stringing her along. I thought if she believed I would join with her then I could find a way to *trap* her. I wasn't expecting her to bring me here though!" said Valentina.

"It's true!" Golden Briar agreed. "I didn't want Valentina to meet her at first, but she insisted."

"I was sure I could find a way to stop her," said Valentina.

"Oh," said Isla, realising she had misjudged

her. "I should have trusted you."

"Yes, you really should've!" said Valentina. She turned to Prancer. "Do you know where my aunt is imprisoned, Prancer?"

"Ms Willow shut her and her unicorn in a shed in the grounds of the academy before transporting them here to a cave in the woods. I can show you the way there. Get on my back, Isla – it'll be faster if you ride."

Hardly able to believe her eyes, Isla scrambled off the ice and on to Prancer's back. She'd never ridden another unicorn before and tall, strong Prancer felt very different from little Buttercup. Isla's heart twisted. She wished Buttercup was there with her. *But at least she's not in danger,* she consoled herself as they began to gallop around the lagoon. She cursed herself for not trusting Valentina earlier and for not having told the teachers

about Ms Willow when she'd had the chance. She shouldn't have worried about looking silly. She should have just burst into the staffroom. She glanced behind her, half expecting to see Ms Willow racing after them.

After a few minutes, Prancer skidded to a stop. "Ms Nettles and Thyme are in that cave," she hissed, motioning towards an opening in the grey stone in front of them.

Three wolves were guarding the entrance. They lowered their heads and began to snarl. Their eyes glowed red.

"Ms Willow has enchanted them to attack anyone who gets too close," warned Prancer.

"Can you lift the enchantment?" asked Valentina.

"Not on my own. It takes both a spell-weaving unicorn and their partner to undo enchantment spells."

The wolves inched forward, their eyes

fixed on the unicorns, their wide open mouths revealing razor-sharp teeth.

Isla saw the wolves' muscles bunch. They were about to spring! She tensed, and then suddenly a little unicorn came bursting out of the nearby trees and charged recklessly at the wolves.

"Buttercup!" Isla shrieked, her head spinning. Whatever was her unicorn doing there?

"I won't let you hurt Isla! I won't!" whinnied Buttercup, fiercely galloping straight towards the snarling wolves!

CHAPTER TEN

The lead wolf leapt at Buttercup. Isla screamed as she saw its open mouth and its sharp fangs, but a second later it was flying sideways through the air. It landed with a howl, Freya and Honey standing beside it. Using Honey's super-speed, they'd galloped flat out into the wolf, knocking it off target. Buttercup was safe from the wolf – for now!

"Way to go, Freya and Honey!" cried Rosa as she appeared from the trees with Violet, Ariana and Matilda.

"Isla! I'm so glad you're all right," Buttercup

said, racing over to her. "We were in the barn when I heard you shout at Valentina outside. When I went to the door I saw you running towards the lake. I galloped after you and got there just as you grabbed Valentina and disappeared with her and Ms Willow! What's going on?"

"Oh, Buttercup!" Isla jumped from Prancer to bury her face in Buttercup's mane. "Thank you for coming after me." Being with her unicorn, that was all that mattered!

"I always want to be by your side when you're in danger," said Buttercup.

"And I want to be by yours," said Isla hugging her.

Ariana's voice brought her back to reality. "You've done it, Whisper!"

Glancing round, Isla saw that Whisper had used her calming magic to free the wolves. The red had died from their eyes and they were now

slinking away, shaking their heads as if they were dazed. The others crowded round, congratulating Whisper.

"Come on, Golden Briar!" cried Valentina. "We need to free my aunt!"

As Golden Briar cantered towards the cave, Matilda squealed, "Isla, you and Buttercup have bonded!"

Buttercup excitedly nuzzled Isla's head. "She's right. You've got a streak of pink, yellow and green in your hair. The same colours as my mane!"

Isla felt like she was going to explode with happiness as she and Buttercup hugged. "I still don't understand how you got here to the lagoon," she said.

"We guessed Ms Willow had taken you here," said Matilda.

"Buttercup and Crystal worked together, combining Buttercup's finding magic with

Crystal's snow magic and making the coolest snow twister ever!" said Rosa. "We weren't sure if it was going to work but the twister was like a massive tornado. It followed Buttercup's magical arrow and brought us to these woods."

"We didn't know where we were and then you suddenly appeared with Valentina, Golden Briar and Prancer!" said Ariana. "So, what happened to you?"

Isla and Prancer quickly explained.

"I'm free now. I don't have to do what Ms Willow says any more," said Prancer, delightedly.

"Hey, everyone!" Valentina called from the cave entrance. "My aunt and Thyme are inside but I can't wake them up."

"They're under a spell," said Prancer. "If we take them back to the academy, one of the teachers should know enough about spells to work with me to lift the enchantment."

Isla and Buttercup

"Let's go!" said Rosa.

"NO!" screamed a voice. There was a flash of light and a bolt of magic came shooting towards them. The unicorns leapt out of the way just in time.

"I never should have trusted you!" Ms Willow hissed at Valentina.

"Move, Golden Briar!" Valentina screamed as Ms Willow threw a firebolt at them.

"I've got this!" Golden Briar slammed his hooves on the ground and, calling up his wind magic, he swept the firebolt to one side. It hit the tree and exploded with a terrifying bang. Flames and sparks shot into the air. Isla clutched at Buttercup's mane as they were blown sideways, crashing into Pearl. Another firebolt spun from Ms Willow's hand. Golden Briar forced that one away too. The trees swayed, their branches creaking and groaning in the wind.

"Everyone, over here," shrieked Violet. "Let Twinkle protect you."

Twinkle had conjured a shimmering dome of starlight. It rose over him like a curved shield. Buttercup ducked behind it, along with the other unicorns and their riders.

CRACK! CRASH! BANG!

The firebolts came fast and furious, hitting the shield and pinging off in all directions. Nearby bushes and trees burst into flames. Ms Willow's face screwed up and she flung her hands to the sky. A black bolt of lightning forked down and slammed into the shield. It buckled and bent.

Twinkle half closed his eyes as he tried desperately to keep the shield in place.

"Keep going, Twinkle," urged Violet, stroking his neck.

"I can't hold it for much longer." Twinkle was gasping with the effort. "We need a new plan."

Ms Willow cackled and an arrow of dark magic whizzed towards them, black smoke trailing in its wake. It speared the dome at its centre. There was a loud pop and the shield collapsed.

"It's over!" Ms Willow said, sneering. "Bind them!" She pointed at the unicorns.

From the pockets of her cloak silver ribbons came slithering like evil snakes. They raced across the ground towards the unicorns.

"Keep clear of the binding ribbons!" cried Prancer anxiously. "If they wrap around you, you'll be under Ms Willow's control!"

"Use your magic, Golden Briar!" cried Valentina.

Golden Briar stamped his hooves. A wind swept the ribbons straight into the branches of a tree.

Ms Willow snarled in fury and hurled another ball of magic at Golden Briar.

BANG! As the magic exploded, Golden Briar

reeled backwards, the wind dropped and the ribbons fell to the ground. They began to slither towards the unicorns again.

Valentina threw her arms round Golden Briar's neck. "Try again! You can do it, Golden Briar. Trust me, you're brilliant."

Golden Briar arched his neck proudly and banged his hooves down. The wind tore through the trees and swept the ribbons back – straight towards Ms Willow.

"No!" she said, gasping and attempting to hurl another spell at Golden Briar, but it was too late. The ribbons were already winding around her. They surged over her, rapidly encircling her until she was almost completely covered.

"Oh wow, Golden Briar!" squealed Valentina. "Look what you did!"

With a roar, Pearl transformed into a sabre-toothed polar bear and leapt on to Ms Willow,

pinning her down to stop her wriggling away like a silver slug.

"What should we do with her?" Matilda yelled from Pearl's back.

"I'll use my spell-weaver magic to transport her to Unicorn Academy," whinnied Prancer. "The teachers can help me from there. With Ms Willow a prisoner and unable to do bad magic, the island will be safe again. After that, I shall find my real

owner, Lacey. I've missed her so much. Thank you for freeing me!" Tossing her magnificent mane back, she trotted over and touched her face to Ms Willow's head. There was a flash and the two of them vanished.

"We did it!" said Ariana looking stunned. "We actually caught Ms Willow. The island is safe again!"

Golden Briar nuzzled Valentina's neck. "I hope Prancer reunites with her real owner. It must be awful for them both to have been separated," she said. "I can't imagine not being with you, Valentina."

"It would be the worst feeling in the world," agreed Valentina, hugging him.

"Valentina you've bonded! There's a golden streak in your hair!" cried Isla, pointing. Valentina grabbed a strand of her long brown hair and, seeing the golden streak, she burst into happy

tears. "Now we can graduate!" she cried.

"We're all going to graduate together!" cried Rosa. "Hip hip hooray!" she whooped. The others joined in and for a few wonderful moments the dark trees rang with the sound of their cheers.

CHAPTER ELEVEN

As the cheers faded, Violet was struck by a worrying thought. "How are we going to get back to the academy?"

"I can try conjuring a twister again," said Crystal eagerly. She stamped a hoof.

A few pink sparks flew up into the air, turning into pink snowflakes. They swirled together in a small tornado. "It's much too small," said Crystal in dismay. "Making such a huge twister before must have worn my magic out."

"Don't worry," Rosa comforted her unicorn. "You did brilliantly just to get us here. We'll find

another way to get home."

They all exchanged looks. No one wanted to be the one to say it but how were they going to do that?

"Girls?"

They swung round. Ms Nettles was standing in the cave entrance, swaying slightly, her glasses sitting at a wonky angle on her nose. Her unicorn, Thyme, was standing beside her, yawning sleepily.

"Whatever's going on?" Ms Nettles demanded, taking her glasses off and rubbing her eyes.

"You're awake, Aunt!" said Valentina,

looking relieved. "Are you all right?"

"The bad magic must be fading. Prancer said the island would be safe again with Ms Willow a prisoner!" Isla said.

Ms Nettles blinked. "The last thing I remember is heading off to a meeting about Ms Willow now a Whatever is going on?"

The girls quickly told her what had happened.

As they talked, Ms Nettles' eyes grew wider and wider. "Well, I never! You really freed Prancer and captured Ms Willow?"

"Yes," said Valentina. She smiled at her aunt. "I'm so glad you're OK. When Ms Willow told me she'd kidnapped you, I was really worried."

"You have a good heart, Valentina," said Ms Nettles, smiling back. "Even if it has been buried under a slightly questionable attitude at times. But I've always had faith in you and..." Her smile broadened as her eyes fell on the golden streak in

Valentina's hair. "It appears I was right. You have finally bonded with Golden Briar."

Valentina beamed. "Isla and Buttercup have bonded too. We can all graduate – so long as we can get back to the academy in time."

"Can you help us?" Ariana asked Ms Nettles anxiously.

"Thyme does not have transporting powers," said Ms Nettles. "However, I have an idea. You say the Frozen Lagoon is on the other side of the trees? And underneath its surface there is all the magic that Ms Willow has stolen from the island?"

They nodded.

Ms Nettles vaulted onto Thyme. "Then maybe the island magic can help us. Come with me – there's no time to waste!"

They followed Ms Nettles through the trees.

"If my plan succeeds then by working as a team we can return to the academy *and* release

the stored magic back to where it belongs," Ms Nettles explained over her shoulder.

Isla felt her stomach twist with excitement. What were they going to do?

They reached the Frozen Lagoon and followed Ms Nettles on to the thick ice. Underneath the surface the multi-coloured magic bubbled as if it was desperate to be free. The unicorns slipped and slid but they kept on going until they reached the very centre of the lagoon.

"Stand in a circle, everyone. Now hold hands," said Ms Nettles. "If we all unite, I believe we can direct our unicorns' magic into something different from their usual powers. Unicorns, you must touch each other too, and everyone must focus on melting the ice."

"Melting the ice?" said Valentina. "But won't we drown?"

"Trust the island to look after us," said Ms

Nettles confidently. "Amazing magical feats can be achieved through love and faith. With your love of each other –" her look took in all the girls and their unicorns – "and your love of the island, we can do this. Are you ready?"

Everyone nodded.

"Then form a circle. Unicorns, call up your magic and focus on what you want it to do!"

The unicorns stood shoulder to shoulder, their

muzzles touching as they drummed their hooves on the ice.

Melt the ice, melt the ice, thought Isla, concentrating hard. To her astonishment, sparks flew up from the unicorns' hooves and joined together above their heads in a ball of glittering light.

"Keep going, everyone!" urged Ms Nettles.

Isla's mind filled with pictures of the ice melting. She felt Buttercup trembling as she conjured every bit of magic she could.

A bright pink star suddenly shot from the glittering ball, then another and another, until suddenly there was a great fountain of stars shooting into the sky. They whizzed through the air and landed on the ice.

CRACK! CRACK! CRACK!

As the stars fell, a spiderweb spread across the icy surface and the magic water began to bubble up from underneath. The only solid ice was the

circle the unicorns were standing on. More stars shot out as the icy lagoon split into fragments and melted away. The water rushed faster, swirling round the girls and unicorns on their island of ice, rising higher but not touching them. Suddenly, it exploded over the banks of the lagoon, flowing away in multicoloured streams and rivulets. The water was returning the magic to where it belonged.

"We've done it!" cried Ms Nettles triumphantly. "Now, Crystal, try using your magic to make a twister again. I am sure the island will help us."

Crystal slammed her hooves down on the ice and an enormous twister of pink snowflakes whooshed around them. "It's working!" she whinnied as the twister suddenly swept them all away.

★

There was a lot of explaining to do when they

got back to the academy. The other teachers were delighted and very relieved to see the girls, unicorns and Ms Nettles back safe and sound, and to catch up on what had been happening. The girls heard that Ms Willow had been bound by magic and taken away to prison. She would never be able to cast spells again.

The next day, when the girls woke up, everywhere seemed to glimmer and shine more brightly than ever before, as if the beautiful island was rejoicing at having its magic back. The morning was spent grooming and bathing their unicorns and packing their bags, and after lunch everyone's parents started to arrive for graduation. They toured the school and stables, admiring the decorations and Matilda's mural, before it was time for each dorm to do a riding display.

Isla's heart jittered inside her chest as she waited at the edge of the arena on Buttercup.

The unicorns' coats shone and the sparkly ribbons plaited through their manes and tails looked beautiful. Ruby dorm was on first and the parents clapped loudly as Buttercup found various things hidden around the arena that Golden Briar then transported back to Valentina with her wind magic. Anna's unicorn Lumiere performed an amazing light display accompanied by a lively polka tune from Molly's unicorn, Sparkle.

Next it was the turn of Diamond dorm. Isla clapped enthusiastically as Honey thrilled everyone with demonstrations of her super-speed, Pearl used a glamour to turn into a snarling tiger and Whisper soothed her with calming magic. Then Crystal carried everyone to the centre of the arena in a snow twister, where Twinkle covered them with a glittering translucent shield.

Isla and Buttercup

The riding displays were followed by the actual graduation ceremony. As darkness fell, students and unicorns filed into the ballroom to huge applause from the parents and teachers.

"Stay back, give us some space so my parents can see me properly," Valentina hissed as Buttercup trotted up behind Golden Briar.

Isla grinned, "That's the bossy Valentina we know and love," she whispered to Buttercup. Valentina had softened a lot over the year but it was clear that her snooty, aloof side hadn't left her. Isla didn't mind. Valentina had more than proved that her heart was in the right place.

As Ms Nettles started her speech, Isla looked round at her friends and thought how much she was going to miss them. They would definitely keep in touch, though. Violet had already arranged a sleepover at her house. Ms Nettles' voice broke into Isla's thoughts.

Isla and Buttercup

"Graduating students and unicorns, the staff and I are very proud of your achievements. You came here as strangers and leave as lifelong friends. Wherever you go on the island, know that your friends are with you." Ms Nettles paused as everyone cheered and clapped. "And now," she said, as silence fell again. "Please come forward and collect your scrolls."

Isla was so thrilled to receive her graduation scroll that, when she'd shaken hands with Ms Nettles and Ms Rosemary, she turned to wave it at her own and Buttercup's parents.

"Party time!" said Buttercup as they filed off the stage.

The ballroom was hung with snowflakes and the long tables piled high with so much delicious food – tiny sandwiches, chocolate cakes, plates of unicorn-shaped biscuits, fruit platters and a huge sugar unicorn. Some of

the students and unicorns danced whilst others talked or gathered around the table, eating and drinking.

Isla and Diamond dorm took plates heaped with treats outside to the banks of the lake. The rainbow-coloured water shone in the moonlight and, behind the lake, the marble school buildings were silhouetted against the star-studded sky.

"It's so beautiful," said Rosa. "I'm glad we managed to stop Ms Willow. Just imagine if she'd captured all our unicorns."

"It would have been awful," Ariana said softly.

Violet smiled at Isla. "I'm so happy we graduated together."

Isla nodded, her hands playing in Buttercup's long silky mane. "And Valentina, too." She looked over to where Valentina was joining in

the dancing with Golden Briar.

"Yes," said Matilda. "She's changed a lot this year."

"We all have," said Violet thoughtfully. "But isn't that part of being at Unicorn Academy? To learn about our unicorns and ourselves?"

"I'm going to miss it," said Isla softly. "And all of you."

"Don't get sad now," said Matilda quickly. "There's Violet's sleepover to look forward to, remember?"

"And we're going to holiday together every summer!" said Freya.

They all smiled.

"Just think how good our magic will be by next summer after we've practised some more!" said Buttercup.

Isla hugged her. "Your magic is really good already. I'm sorry I ever doubted you. When

you asked it to find Ms Willow and it took us to Ms Nettles in the shed you were right. It was Ms Willow in disguise!"

"Everyone's magic has been useful," said Rosa. "We worked as a team."

"Because that's when unicorns and their riders are strongest," said Buttercup, looking at Isla through her eyelashes.

Violet smiled at Twinkle. "You know, I think that might be the most important lesson of all." There was a whizzing noise and a bang and the sky was suddenly filled with pink and purple stars.

"Fireworks!" Rosa gasped.

More and more fireworks shot into the air and filled the sky until a final one formed the figure of a rearing unicorn.

Everyone clapped and cheered once more. Isla wrapped her arms around Buttercup's

neck, her heart swelling as she watched the rearing unicorn shining high above them. She'd bonded with Buttercup, she'd just graduated and she'd had the best year of her life.

"I'm so glad you're my unicorn," she told Buttercup. "From now on, I'm definitely going to be more like you. I'll believe in myself and be braver, and most of all I'm going to speak out instead of worrying that people might think I'm stupid."

Buttercup blew on her hair. "Well, I'm going to try to be more like *you* and think more before I jump in. Maybe attacking an enchanted wolf on my own wasn't the most sensible thing to do!"

Isla giggled and buried her face in Buttercup's mane, breathing in her sweet unicorn smell. "We'll work together to protect Unicorn

Island," she vowed.

"And each other," said Buttercup, her dark eyes shining with love.

"Always," said Isla, with a smile.